Frozen Noses

Frozen Noses

by JAN CARR

illustrated by
DOROTHY DONOHUE

SCHOLASTIC INC.
New York Toronto London Auckland Sydney
Mexico City New Delhi Hong Kong

ISBN 0-439-17207-1

Text copyright © 1999 by Jan Carr.
Illustrations copyright © 1999 by Dorothy Donohue. All rights reserved.
Published by Scholastic Inc., 555 Broadway, New York, NY 10012, by arrangement
with Holiday House, Inc. SCHOLASTIC and associated logos are trademarks
and/or registered trademarks of Scholastic Inc.

12 11 10 9 8 7   2 3 4 5 6/0

Printed in the U.S.A.   09

First Scholastic printing, January 2001

Book design by Sylvia Frezzolini Severance

For Charlie, who was born in a light flurry of snow,
and for Mom, who shines in winter
— J. C.

To my buddy Janet,
to Regina for her trust,
and in memory of my sweet Megga May
— D. D.

Frozen noses
Tingly toeses

Sniffle, snuffle
Winter's cold!

Better bundle!
Quiver, shiver
Booted, buckled
Buttonholed

Snowballs, throw balls
Pack and stack them
Roly-poly
Chubby chap

Coal for eyes
A proper topper
Whoosh of wind
Whoa! Catch that hat!

Onward! Upward!
I'm a climber!
Scramble up
Heave-ho the rope!

Veer down, steer down
Whee, I'm whizzing!
Thump a-bump
The slippery slope

Lace my skates up
Tie them tightly
Ready, steady
I won't fall

Slide, collide
Get good at gliding
Hit a skid
Whoops! All a-sprawl!

Sun sets early
Sky's a-swirly
Clouds collect–
Another storm?

Bundle blankets
Crackle, kindle
Cup of cocoa–

Winter warm.